The Adventures Of the
Bugtussle Bunch

Tales of the Mystic Tree House

By RR Hover

Copyright © 2011 by R.R. Hover

All rights reserved. No part of this publication may be reproduced, distributed, or transmitted in any form or by any means, including photocopying, recording, or other electronic or mechanical methods, without the prior written permission of the publisher, except in the case of brief quotations embodied in critical reviews and certain other noncommercial uses permitted by copyright law. For permission requests, write to the Author, addressed "Attention: Permissions Coordinator," at the address below.

Ronald R. Hover

c/o Hover Enterprises, LLS

2860 Conestoga Court

Alpine, CA 91901

T-619-722-1364 FAX 619-722-1365

E-MAIL rh@hoverenterprises.com

ISBN. 978-09847480-1-3

Dedication

In dedication to my loving sister Patricia "Teda" Hover Benedict I co-dedicate in her memory these creations as my found tribute to my memories of her as we grew up out in the country side together. We lost her to breast cancer and my loving daughters have paid tribute to her memory, as one of many, in several three day Susan G. Komen breast cancer walks in San Diego.

I know she would have loved the characters and adventures as I have depicted them for the reason that we grew up in an old one room country school house, that my parents converted, just across the road from an old civil world dated cemetery of which we used to create spooky adventures. May God Bless and rest her beautiful soul.

I also must give a loving dedication of my creation to my wife and family who are inspiration for the humor, charm and spirit in these works. I'm truly blessed with a loving and devoted wife and a warn, tender and caring family who's closeness is the pride of a fathers heart and a treasure of his legacy. In addition to these traits they are my underlying encouragement and provided for me my true ability to illustrate by my imagination, humor, family pride and enthusiasm they've projected in my life.

At the first bright rays of day break
As shadows slid down ol' Raven Rock
The Bunch devoured buckwheat pancakes
Topped with honey from a wooden crock.

It weren't just an hour before that
they were clad in overalls 'n ol' work clothes
wait'n for that ol' Ruffus the big red rooster
ta commenc'n his wake'um up morn'n crows.

Take'n their last gulps of Gertrude's goat milk
They dashed out the tattered back screen door
They got busy as an ol' pestered bee hive
Hurriedly finish'n their morn'ns daily chores.

Trevor quickly hand milked ol' Betsey
Squirt'n milk in an ol' two gallon wooden pail
Balanced on an ol' three legged milk stool
An dodge'n Betsy's wet fly switch'n tail.

Taylor slop fed the ol' brown sow hog
With twelve pink piglets just run'n round
They oinked, they squealed 'n they grunted
Make'n other contented baby piglet sounds.

Cami broad casted out the Bantys' chicken feed
Ta the peck'n rooster 'n all the chicks 'n lay'n hens
Until Ruffus rooster caught clear site of her
'n quickly chased her clear out the wired pen.

As Brayden fed the two Bluetick coon dogs
'n the slow move'n, floppy eared Blood Hound
A new litter of four frisky Bluetick puppies
Playfully knocked him flat on the...
dog pens ground.

Maci crawled inside the ol' wood hen house
Roll'n out the hens farm fresh large white eggs
Then poured cows' milk in the cats ol' stone bowl
As kittens softly rubbed against her...
skinny l'il legs.

They securely latch-pinned Gertrude's goat pen
Double slide-barred the ol' red barn door
Toss'n fresh hay ta Jasper the ol' gray Jackass
They headed out ta see.... what this new day had
in store.

Stopp'n at a hollowed out tree of Hickory
Inside hung an ol' hemp rope set of stairs
Lead'n up ta a tilted homemade tree house
Survey'n their world on a perch…. way up there.

No one liv'n recalls how the tree house got there
When it was built or who crafted it to fit the tree
And how so strategically 'n tactically it is located
Allow'n a view of Bugtussel Valley in 360 degrees.

The trunk was hollowed out to house the ladder
'n cleverly guard against the sun 'n ol' North Wind
But there remained ol' folk lures 'n wives tales
From ages of ol' bootleggers make'n corn mesh country gin.

But for the Bugtussel Bunch 'n their adventures
It was their complete view of their small world
Where they could scout 'n plan their new ventures
'n let their youthful 'n wild imaginations swirl.

Now, this tree house held very peculiar powers
Magically sail'n them ta lands far unknown
When they held hands 'n wished one wish together
They were carried on a golden winged wish bone.

Their transporter could soar like the swamp eagles
It could glide on the power of up drafts like kites
It could dive like the swamps dart'n Kingfisher
Or do smooth barrel rolls like march's Wood Snipes

It could hover quietly like the mighty fish'n Osprey
'n stand still like the Red Throated Humming Bird
It could do back flips like a graceful fly'n squirrel
'n all its maneuvers controlled with just one word.

But the Bunch vowed to keep that word secret
'n must never be disclosed or made known
The Golden Wishbone runs on sun 'n by wishes
'n without either one it cannot be flown.

Sail'n off ta Enchanted Lake Leprechaun Island
Or Spy'n a-top of ol' sly Bootleggers Ridge
Side track'n away pesky government revenuers
Who hid under the ol' Catatonk Creek Bridge.

Adrift in the mist of thick gray marsh fog
Soar'n high above damp Timber Doodle Swamp
Float'n low over the algae covered Cowards Cove
Where ol' bush whack'n Swamp Pirates stomp.

At times softly land'n in ol' Swamp Fire Bayou's
Where tiny Firefly Fairies ride on calico colored fish
If can you catch one… you best not release him
'til they promise ta grant you…. one big wish.

Measur'n their real world from the tree tops
Or stare'n out at a flock of wild Canadian Geese
While they honked in random while fly'n over
'N were natures surprises never seem ta cease.

Now briefly putt'n all their daydreams behind them
Spy'n out through an ol' hollow swamp reed
Study'n their own homestead stomp'n grounds
From their perch atop that ol' Hickory tree.

They could view the whole town of ol' Bugtussel
The church steeple poke'n up through the soft haze
'n over across ta Brink's green grassy farm meadows
Where the VanVorces' milk cows contently graze.

You could even see clear ta Whitetail Cross'n
Where occasionally grazed allusive Albino deer.
Respected as if their some prized ghostly omens
And from the local hill folks…. they had noth'n ta fear.

As the fog lifted up from the ol' bog ponds
The Bald Eagles 'n Egrets did take ta flight
As morn'n sun rays streamed inta the hollers
The rays golden glows made a mystical sight.

Now there's a crow called ol' Gabby McDermit
Who nested in the Hickory trees highest branch
Warn'n the Bugtussel Bunch when there is trouble
Prevent'n evil predators from have'n a chance.

You'all see that Gabby broke his small right wing
When he was just taken ta flight an learn'n ta fly
They splinted it with two new green willow twigs
Ta no success… but oh how hard they all had tried.

So his home is forever the ol' tree house oak tree
The Bunch brings him bags of food every few day
Their promise to always keep'n him feed 'n healthy
'n his is ta warn harmful 'n evil varmints way.

The oak tree has also be'n home to a variety of other critters
Befriended or helped by this care'n Bugtussel crew
The raccoon named Bandit 'n the red squirrel Rudy
Are merely just ta humbly name but just a few.

Rescued by these five young good Samaritans'
Discovered mostly from their strategic tree house perch
Take'n out time from their chores 'n grand adventures
Alert for critters lost, helpless, hungry or hurt.

They are guardians of the injured 'n helpless
Some orphaned, not able to fend for themselves
Some regard'n the Bunch as their new family
Others headed home when they're healthy 'n well.

Cackle'n back 'n forth ta them when needed
When the Bunch traipses near or traipses afar
From his crows' nest Gabby can easily spot them
Always vigil 'n aware of just where they are.

Now, mischievous Bandit the rascal raccoon
Found with a pickle brine jar stuck on his nose
Now lives in a den of the ol' Hickory tree house
He's a roommate ta ol' Gabby the boisterous crow.

There's Rudy the acrobatic fly'n red squirrel
Had an encounter with a hungry red tailed hawk
Between him 'n his buddy ol' Gabby McDermit
They can conjure up hair rais'n raucous squawks.

But, Rudy has added beneficial talents
He can gracefully glide unnoticed from tree ta tree
Carry'n notes from one kid ta another….when
Separated far from what each other can see.

Then there's Bagger the half blind badger
Woodrow the chunky wishy-washy woodchuck
Philbert the finicky 'n fidgety little brown ferret
'n Mildred the ol' maid meddlesome mallard duck.

There's Wesley the crafty cross eyed weasel
Skippy the spotted three legged pungent skunk
Otto the acrobatic glossy black furred otter
'n Chipper the neighborhoods chatty chipmunk.

There's Grooter the ol' one tooth swamp gator
Greta the gracefully feathered white egret
Harriet the ballerina legged blue feathered heron
'n so many more …you haven't yet met.

But I must now get on with the Bunches story
As they quietly studied 'n pondered ol' Hermits Hill
A mountain hideout from an ol' mystical legend
That its tale gave every child the spooky chills.

It is told that an ol' local hunter 'n fur trapper
Who now lived high in the hills in a hidden cave
That the ol' swamp took his wife 'n his daughter
'n he buried them in a drab watery swamp grave.

The tale was too invite'n for this here young Bunch
They had ta just see things for themselves
Of what had become of the elusive ol' hermit
'n was he really be'n guarded by enchanted elves.

So they had adopted a plan ta try ta uncover
The truth of this ol' re-occurr'n backwoods folklore
'n at last maybe put ta rest once 'n forever
What transpired in the ol' swamp years before.

Now it was early as they trekked up the mountain
The dew on the grass 'n brush was still quite wet
Armed with just knapsacks on ol' walk'n sticks
They made a pledge, 'n the scene was now set.

Vow'n, that if anyone of them was captured
The other three would stay 'n one would flee
Seek'n rescue from home or nearest neighbor
Try'n hard not ta think of what the outcome might be.

Near'n a rocky outcrop that folk lures depicted
Where the cave the ol' Hermit might be found
They crouched low on the top of grayish boulders
Survey'n the land… not make'n the slightest sound.

They spotted white swirl'n smoke from a crevice
Mysteriously emerg'n from a solid rocky ledge
Single file they continued stalk'n on the pathway
They found themselves trapped in a rocky wedge.

Then a ships webbed net fell over the whole bunch
Trevor somehow quickly worked his way free
But before he could completely escaped ta freedom
A rope snare snatched him up in an ol' elm tree.

Then seven little people suddenly encircled them
Carefully uncover'n them 'n bound each one by one
March'n them up the thick paths of the mountain
Guard'n them with what looked like an ol' Blunder
bust pirates gun.

They came ta a tactically arranged maze of timber
Camouflaged with moss 'n green grassy blades
Behind.... where it was so craftily hidden, was
The mouth of a large water carved out cave.

Into the damp dark cave they were ushered
Where lights from oil lamps so dimly glowed
First seated on a bench made of bear rib bones
Then....one by one were commanded where ta go.

Cool clear water dripped from the caves ceil'n.
Stalactites made eerie shadows on the dank walls
The flutter of bat wings shuddered the silence
A screech owl reverberated out spine-chill'n calls.

Just when the cold cave became the darkest
They gradually entered a bright sun-drenched room
Which opened up ta a fresh fragrant garden
With trees 'n brilliant flowers in full bloom.

Side shadows of an ol' man casted uneasiness
As an ol' woman appeared ta their surprise.
A middle aged lady stood quietly behind her
Then seven little people came ta stand by her side.

She then softly asked why they came there
"Are you here ta bring us great harm"
She eased their fears 'n latest scary suspicions
With her quiet reassure'n 'n soft gentle charm.

Explain'n they were just seek'n new adventures
From ol' myths that have long been renowned
The allure of ol' legendary Hermits Mountain
Produced intrigue from ol' stories passed down.

As she went on with her kind interrogations
The shadowy figure slowly appeared in ta site
An elderly gentleman clad in fine tan buck skins
With a long beard 'n hair pure snowy white.

He told them ta sit... he'd tell them the real story
If they'd swear solemn oaths not ta ever repeat
The factual truth behind the ol' false folk fables
'n why they have kept the secrets they keep.

"It was a thick foggy morn in the swamp bog", he stated.
"I was slowly hand pole'n my ol' birch bark canoe
I heard a eerie roar arise out of the cypress trees
What it was I still never actually knew".

"Some say it was a small everglade twister
Or a fierce Devil Wind that wouldn't subside
But it violently destroyed our sturdy log cabin
With my baby girl 'n dear wife trapped inside".

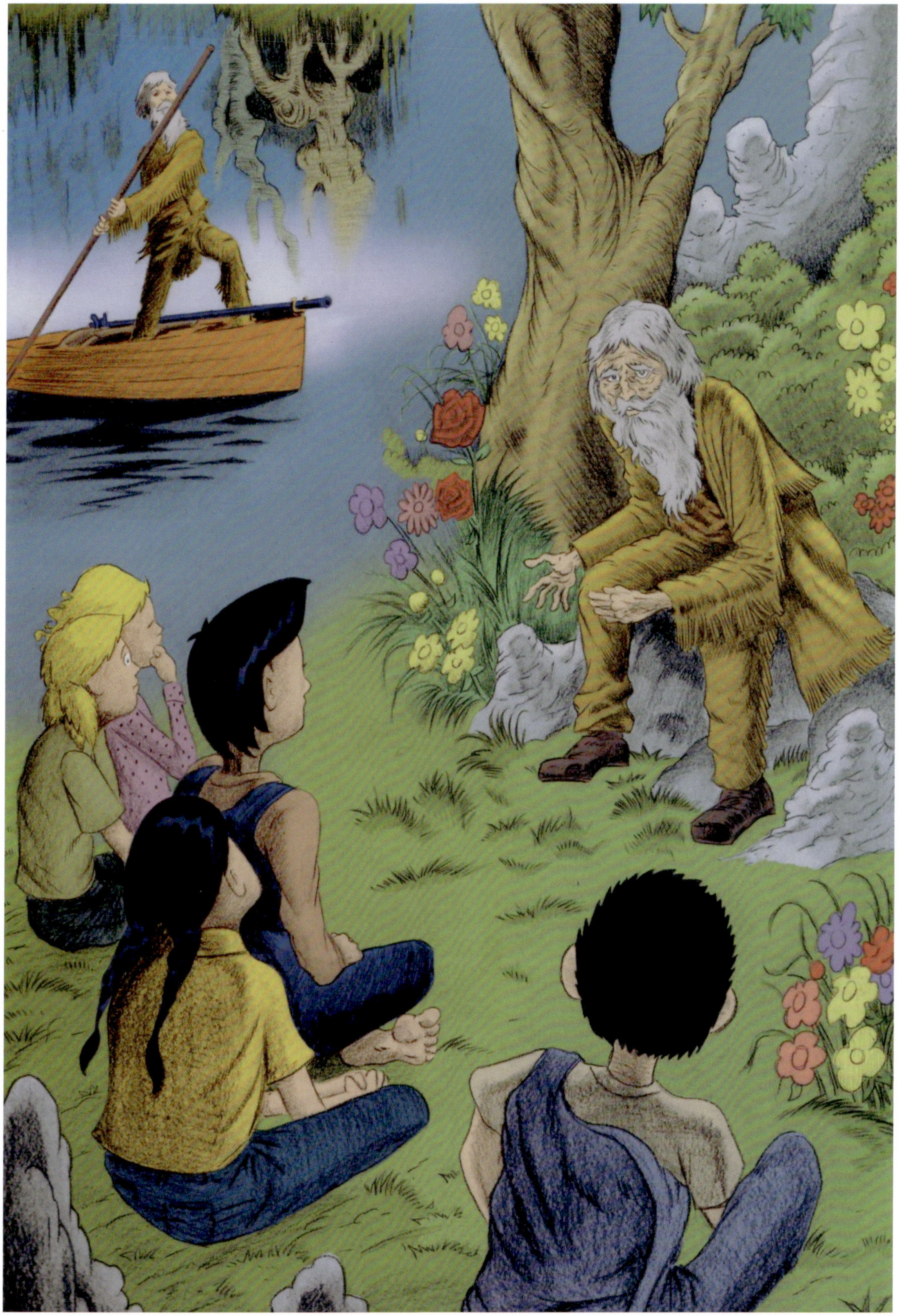

"I frantically poled back ta the destruction
Then my worst fears were harshly realized
They were both gone in a blink of an eyelash
I unselfishly wished it was me that had died".

"I drifted aimlessly through the ol' bayou
With the heavy burden of the loss on my heart
Yet.....how could I go on liv'n without them
With no spirit left.... I had no reason ta start".

"Feel'n a firm tug at the back of my bark boat
I squinted hard through the gray thickened haze
Seven little people carry'n two lifeless objects
It was my wife 'n child...!!! safe 'n just thankfully dazed".

Only catch'n glimpses of them in the swamps mist
Locals labeled the small clan the l'il Mugwhumps
Adapt'n shrewdly into the vast swamps landscape
Blend'n into the foliage 'n by hid'n behind stumps.

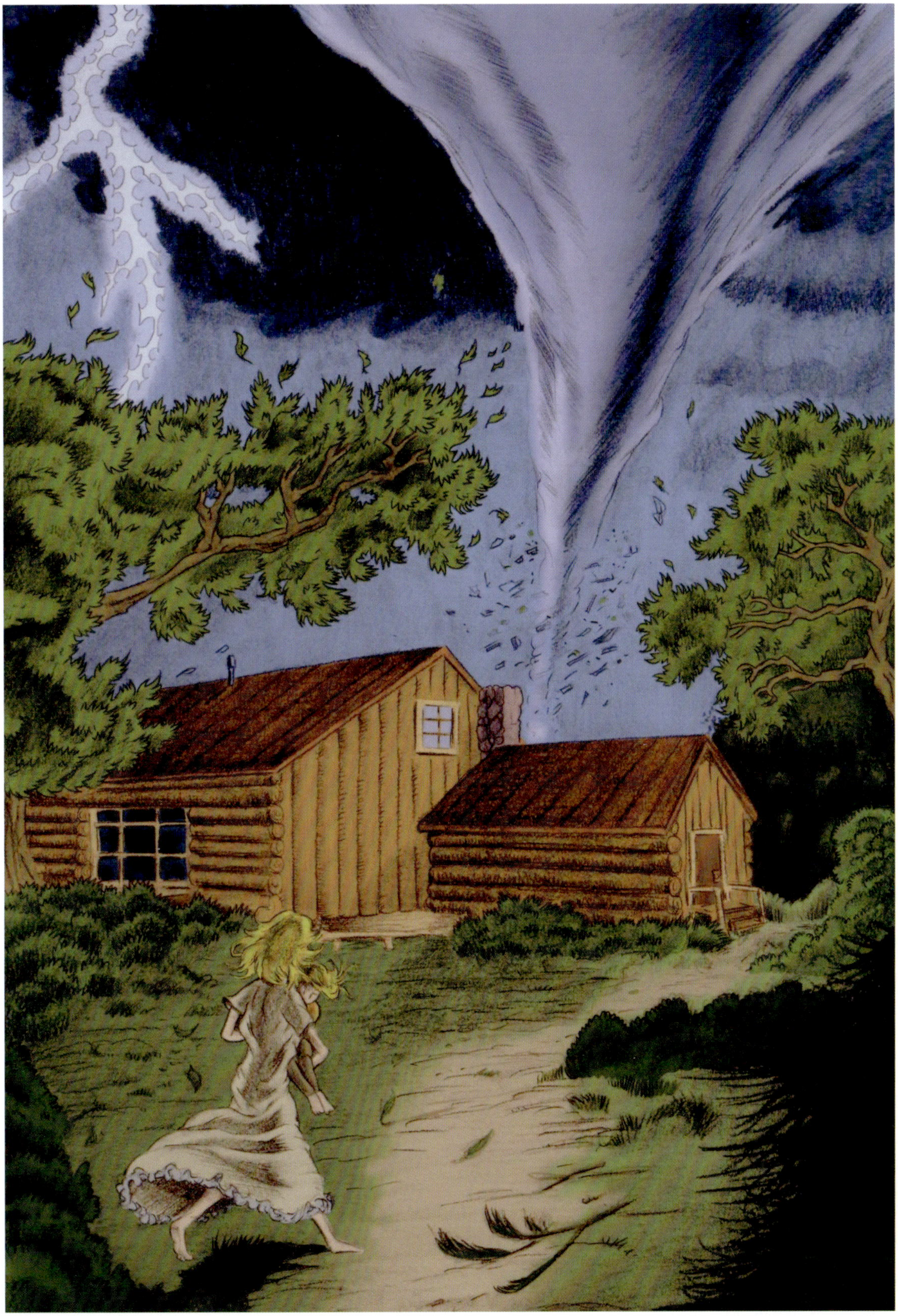

"Rescued by these current kinfolk of l'il swamp people
Haunted by ol' folklores 'n bounties hunters for years
Now endangered by expos'n their recent hideaway
They emerged elf like through my heart broke'n tears".

"Aware what might become of these l'il hero's
Bounty hunters may now well realize they'd saved
My lovely wife 'n precious young daughter
So we made crosses 'n dug nine phony graves".

How the Mugwhumps had come ta ol' Snoggrass
Is as unique as the incredible fables themselves
They were expert cannon tenders on ol' pirate vessels
The pirates alleged they were ol' magical elves.

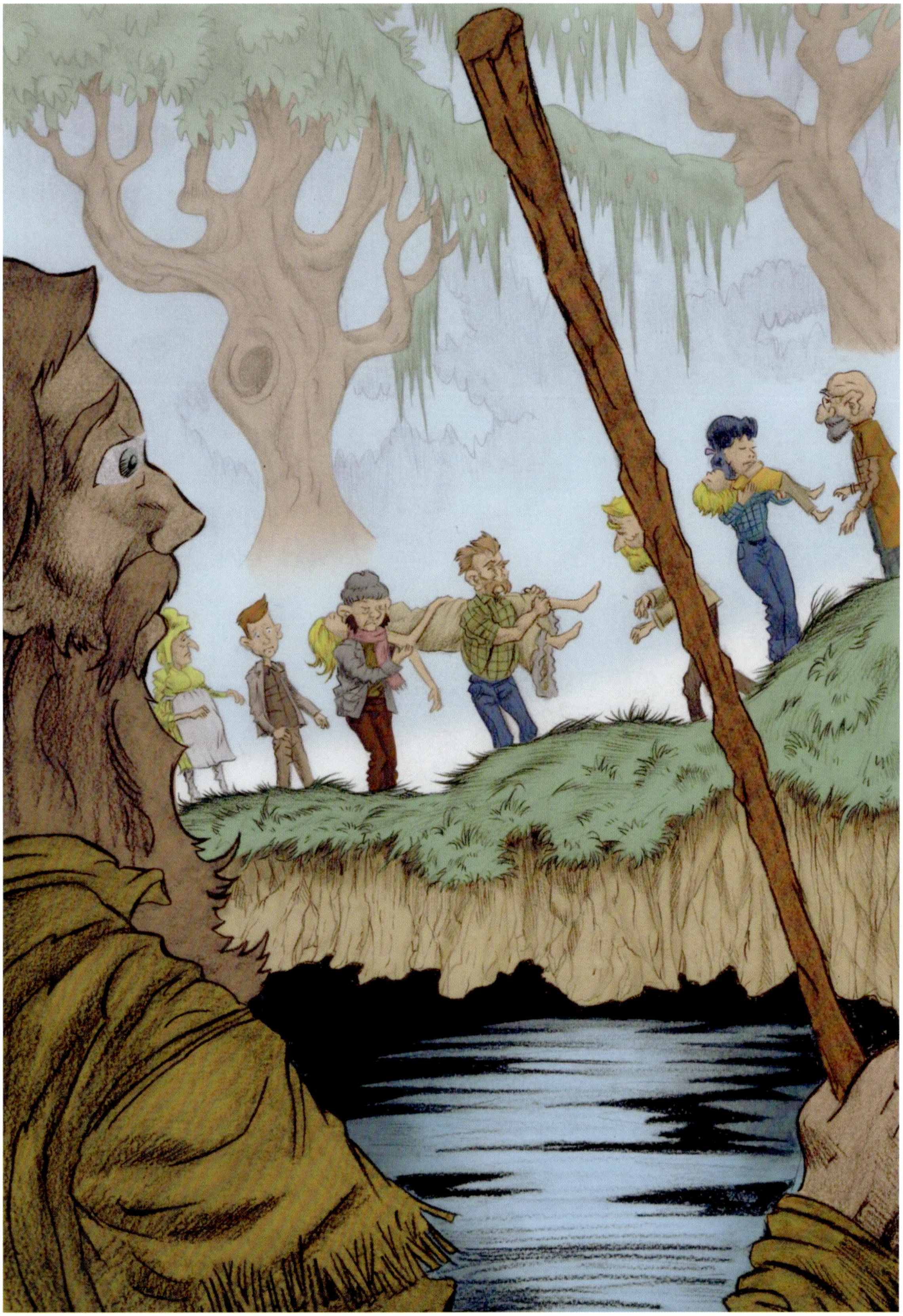

Now years ago….
these wetlands poured out large flows of water
Sufficient ta accommodate 'n buoyed up a flat cargo boat
With a few strong light weight men ta navigate it
Also shrewd enough ta keep men 'n cargo afloat.

The pirates had forcefully seized precious plunder
Desir'n ta bury it where it would be concealed
They knew the perfect tough 'n craftily skilled sailors
Trustworthy ones…
Ones who would never ever reveal.

The Mugwhump couples were perfect candidates
Strong, lightweight, honest 'n courageously bold
Crafty in the ways of shrewdness 'n concealment
'n Carry'n out orders exactly how they're told.

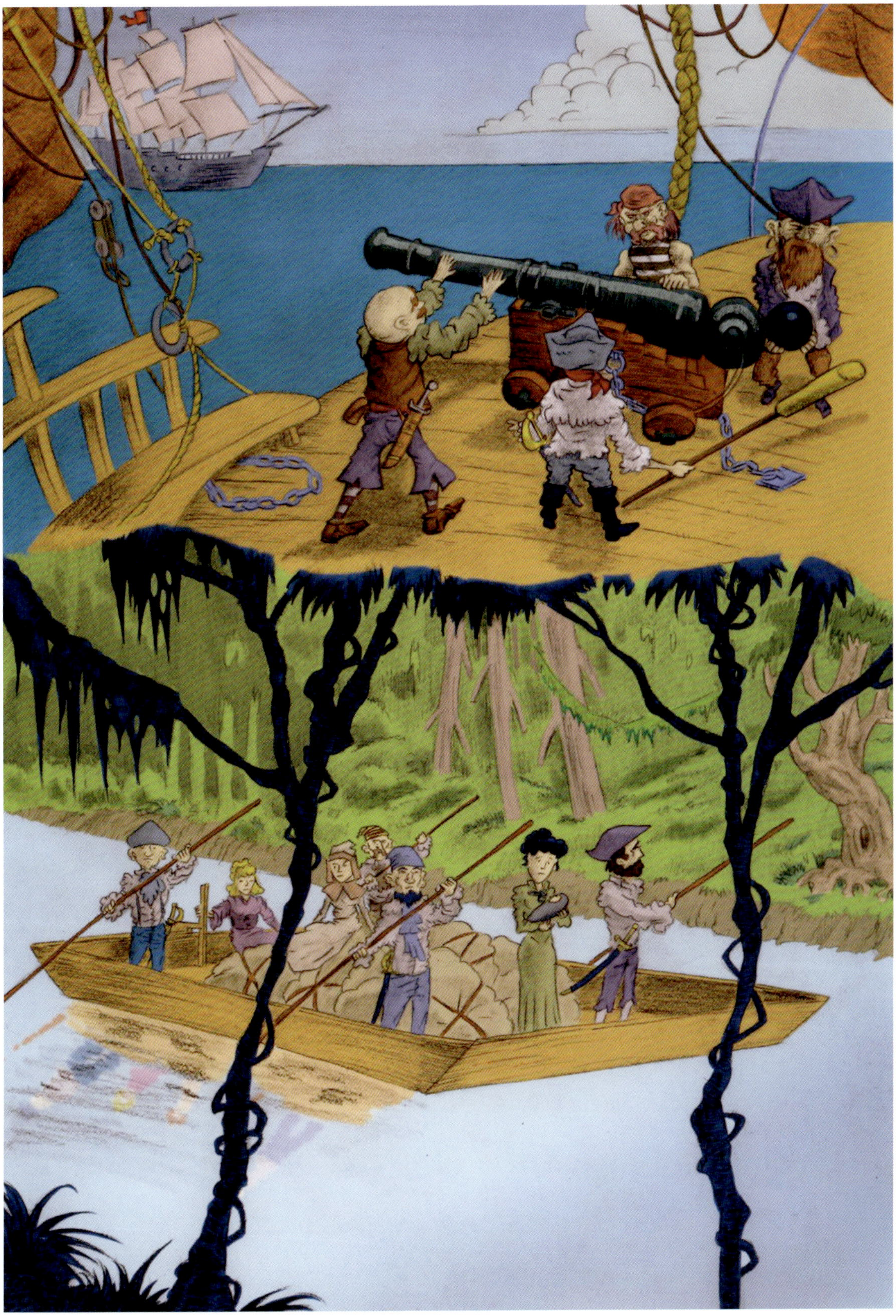

So decades ago...
their ancestors trudged up this watercourse
The stream known then as ol' Snoggrass Run
With the rich bounty they reached ol' Gator Island
Hide'n the plunder... their work was now done.

But a great storm drove their main vessel seaward
Strand'n all Mugwhumps in this ol' marshy land
Settl'n in the shield'n shelter of secluded Snoggrass
Establish'n new futures, new lives 'n new plans.

So over the years they were rarely spotted
Only by ol' trappers, ol' hunters 'n lost hik'n souls
Whenever reports of catch'n glimpses of bog elves
Tales were often doubted but still repeatedly told.

But the lure of ol' rumors of rich treasures
Combined with the ol' myths of safeguard'n elves
Only enhanced the ill greed of treasure seekers
Even if their obsessions might cast on them a spell.

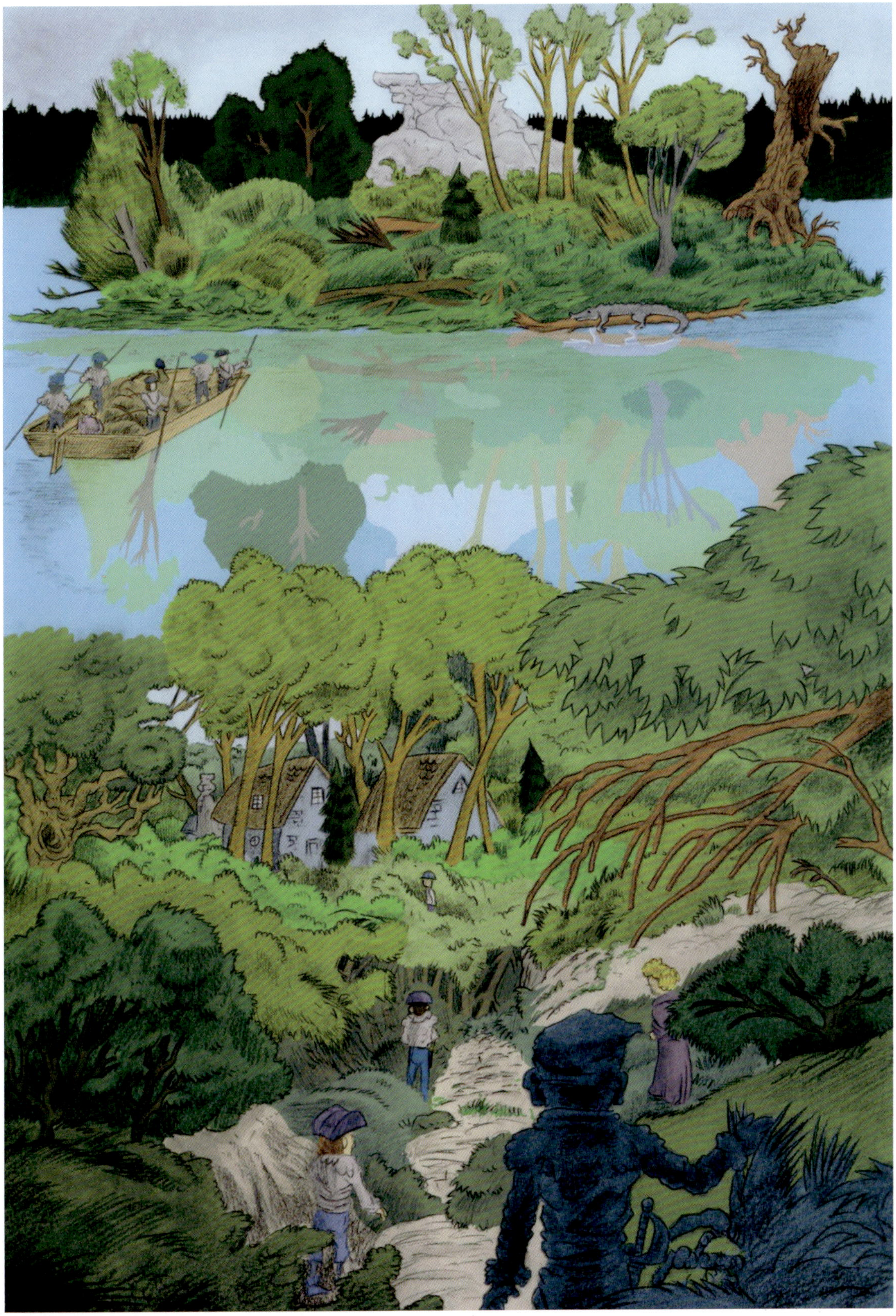

"But while trapp'n I discovered a hide away
High in the vast remote mountains south hills
Gather'n up all our last worldly possessions
We cautiously concealed our tracks with great skills".

"When the cabin debris was finally discovered
All presumed we all were dead 'n at rest
By then we were secure in this safe haven
'n ol' folklores became a part of folks quest".

"You now see why drastic actions were tak'n
In this mountain we're both protected 'n safe
We built this sanctuary not harm'n a soul
'n, no one must never ever discover this place".

"See why we require your oaths 'n your pledges
Ta not tell a soul... not even your close kin
Before we can completely free 'n release you
Of what you saw here 'n where you have been".

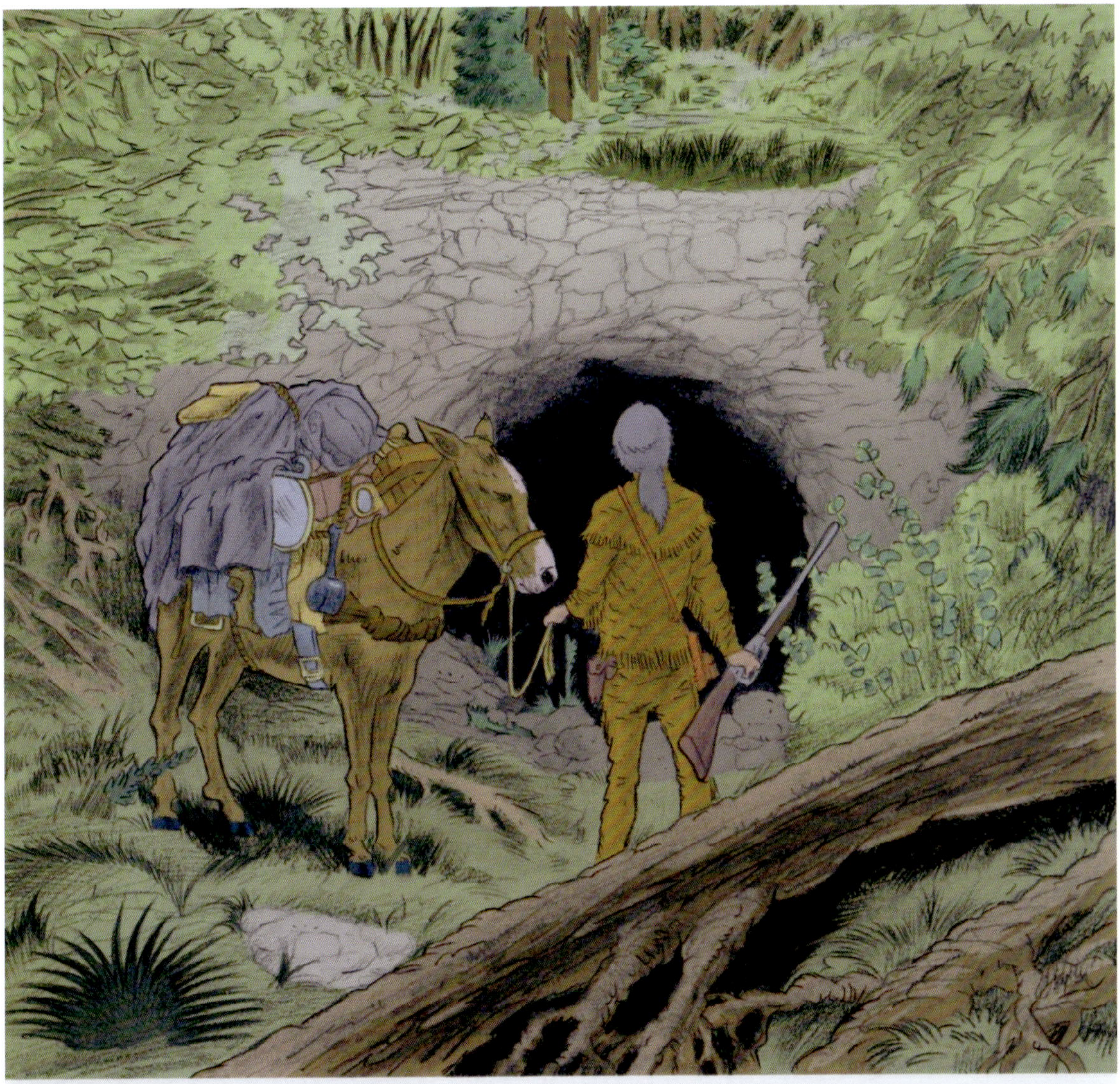
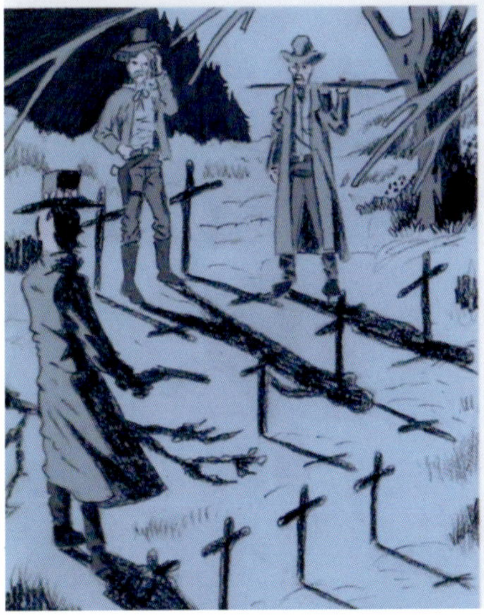
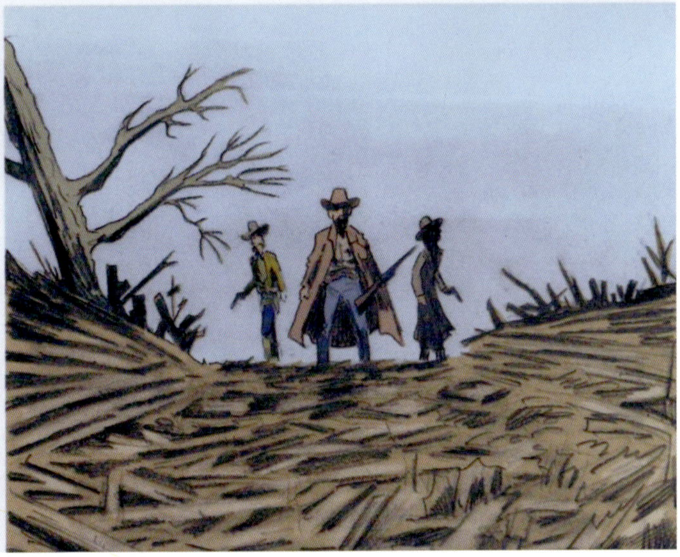

They were in awe of the truths in their story
It all made sense at the way things evolved
They're all thrilled by this blessed conclusion
'n the care'n outcome that God had allowed.

They were unbound 'n served biscuits 'n honey
Give'n nectar drinks from a sweet sugar bush tree
Give'n a tour through this beautifully placed haven
Take'n oaths, they were then kindly set free.

The Hermit said they were welcome ta visit
But cautioned them ta use their God given skills
Not reveal'n where or how they had found them
'n decoy'n others away from their hill.

Trevor politely asked the names of their new friends
One by one they did right proudly proclaim
Start'n first with the chief of this community
Then soundly they all announced their first names.

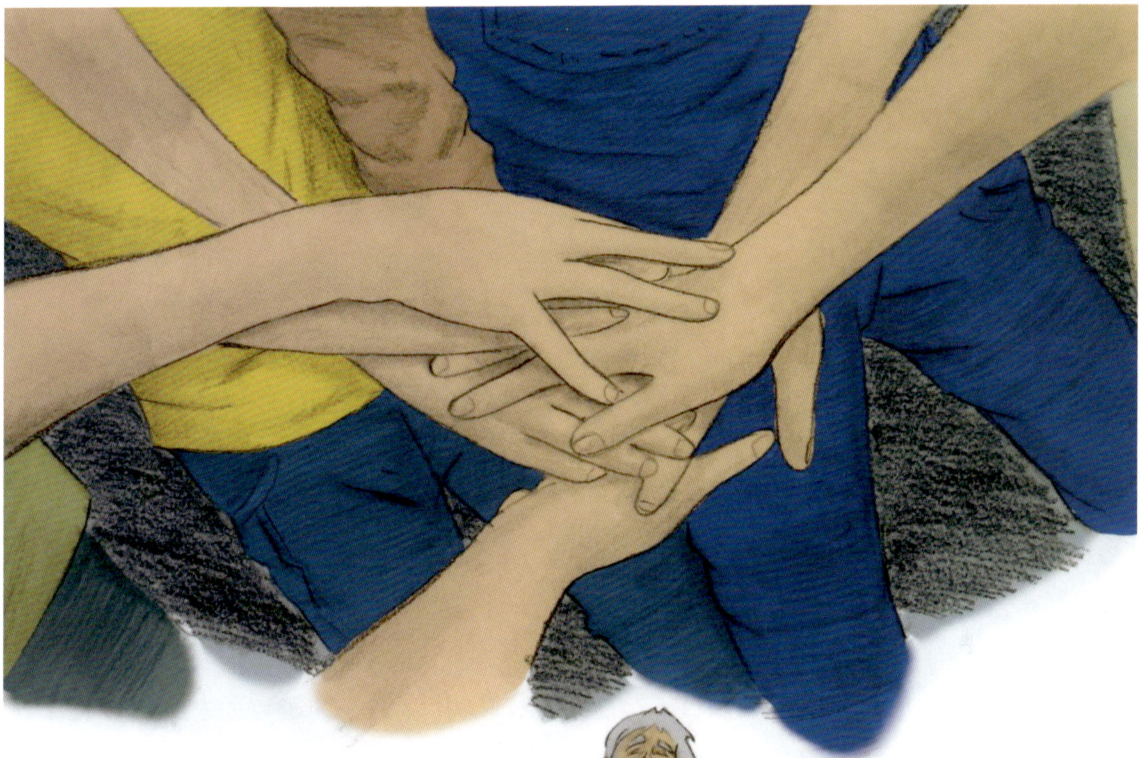

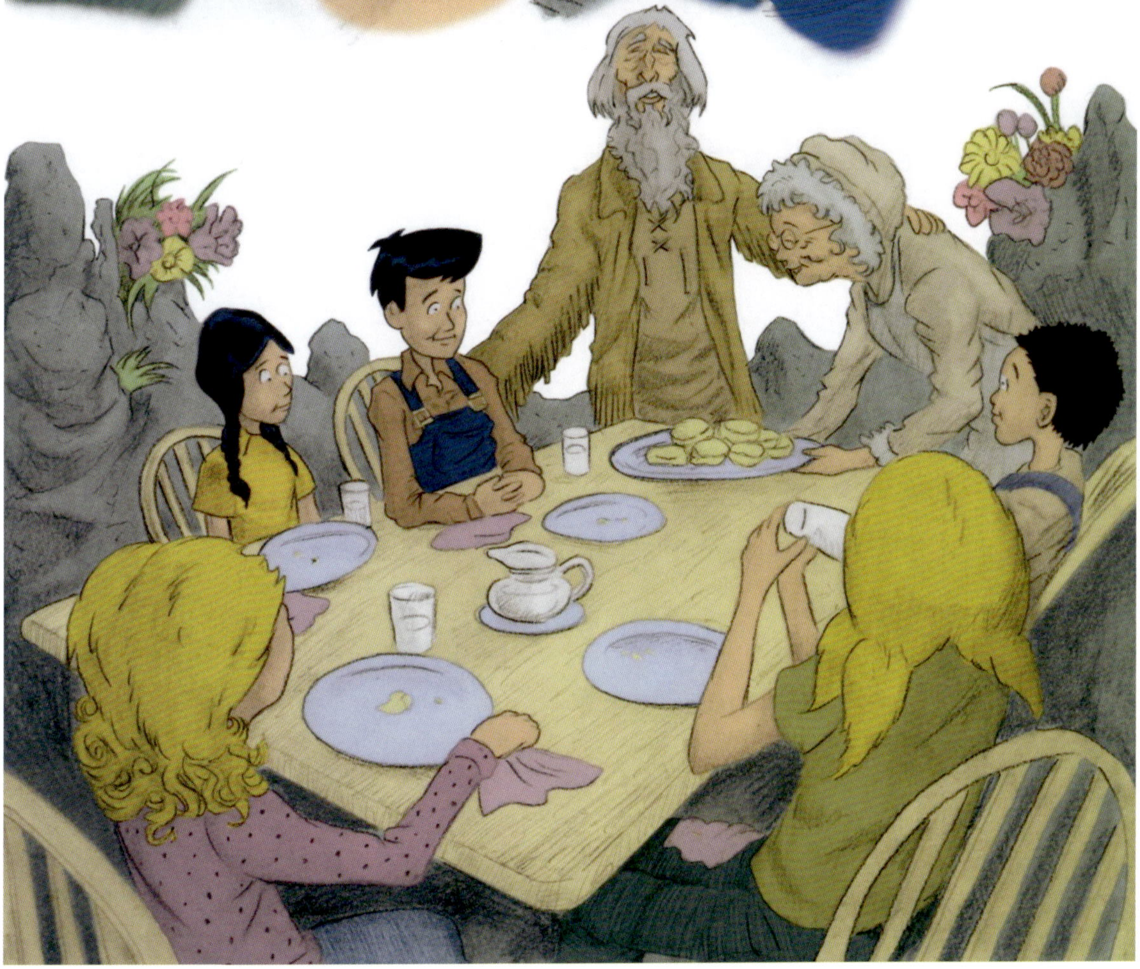

The Hermit declared his sir name as Joshua
The daughter softy said "my names Sarah May"
His wife proclaimed her name was Rebecca Ann
The seven Mugwhumps weren't quite sure what ta say.

So...
The eldest Mugwhump boldly stepped forward
"I'll now introduce them myself one by one,
There's my wife Mary 'n then Caleb my kid brother
'n Joseph, Jeremiah 'n Jabez my three sons."

He loudly boasted himself ta be named Zachariah
As he began announcing his daughter.... he cried
"This girl is my youngest one, Esmeralda (meaning emerald)
This is the first time we introduced ourselves with such pride."

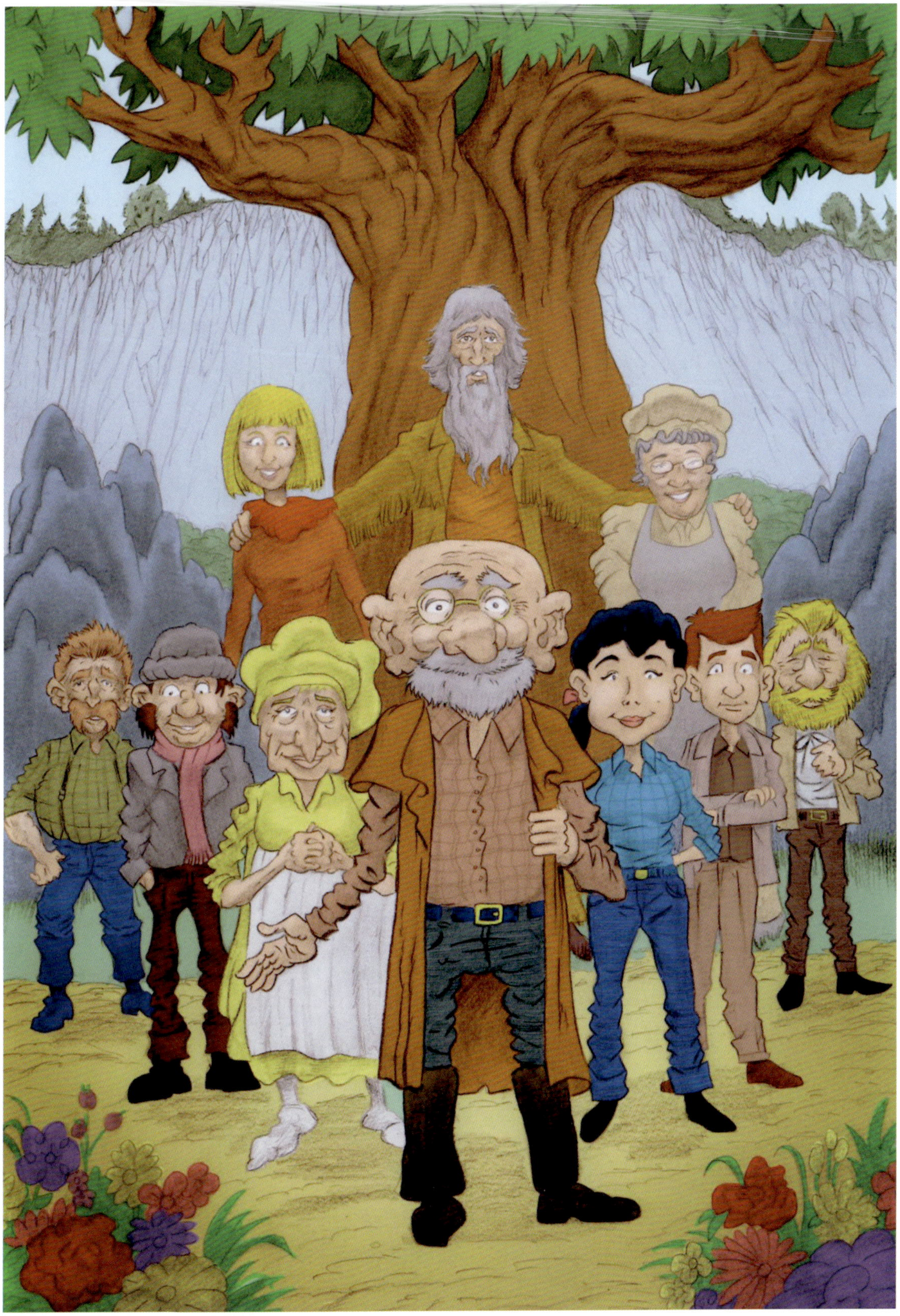

Then....
head'n home with a bitter sweet sendoff
Back track'n their way back down Hermits Hill
Craftily cover'n their tracks as they descended
Quietly share'n 'bout their adventurous thrill.

Safely home they began wash'n up for dinner
Their mothers sternly asked "where have y'all surely been"
They cautiously replied "oh just up in the ol' oak tree house"
As they gave each other... a sly wink 'n mischievous grin.

"We worry....
Y'all hang'n round that ol' rickety tree house
Exaggerate'n, with your imaginations gone wild
Ya'all ought ta start appreciat'n common sense
Like every other respectable hillbilly child".

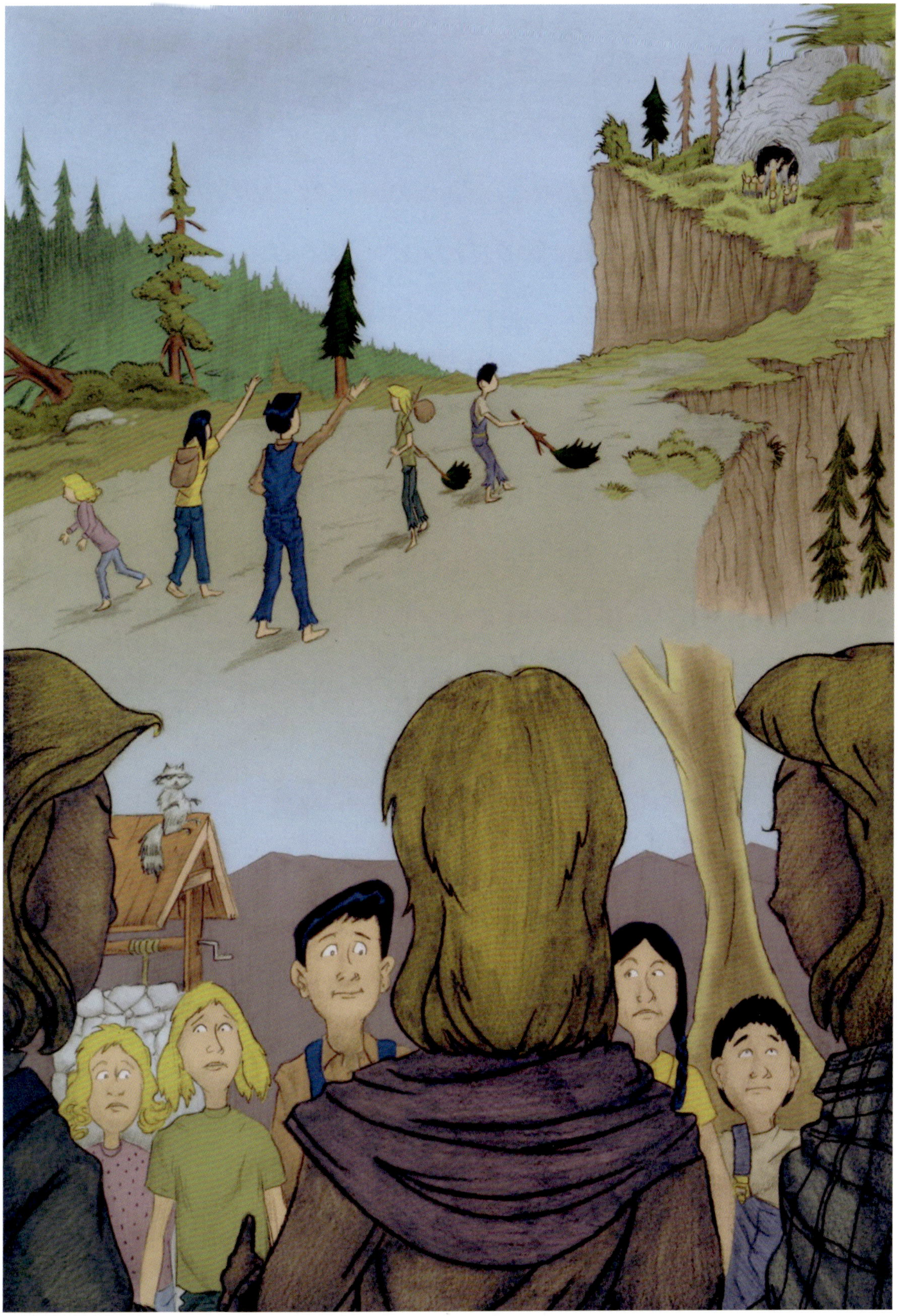

That night as they lay snug in their own beds
Relive'n that days encounter with great care
They couldn't stop think'n 'bout the ol' Hermit's clan
'n how they needed ta say them a prayer.

Whenever they overheard ol' Hermit stories
The Bunch would all gather round with big grins.
'n strongly plead'n ta the folklores story teller
"oh please, please tell us that story again".

With the intrigue of the treasure still haunt'n them
Coupled with their spirit 'n their deep desire ta explore
They started day dream'n 'n plan'n their new venture
'n they just knew time 'll open that new door.

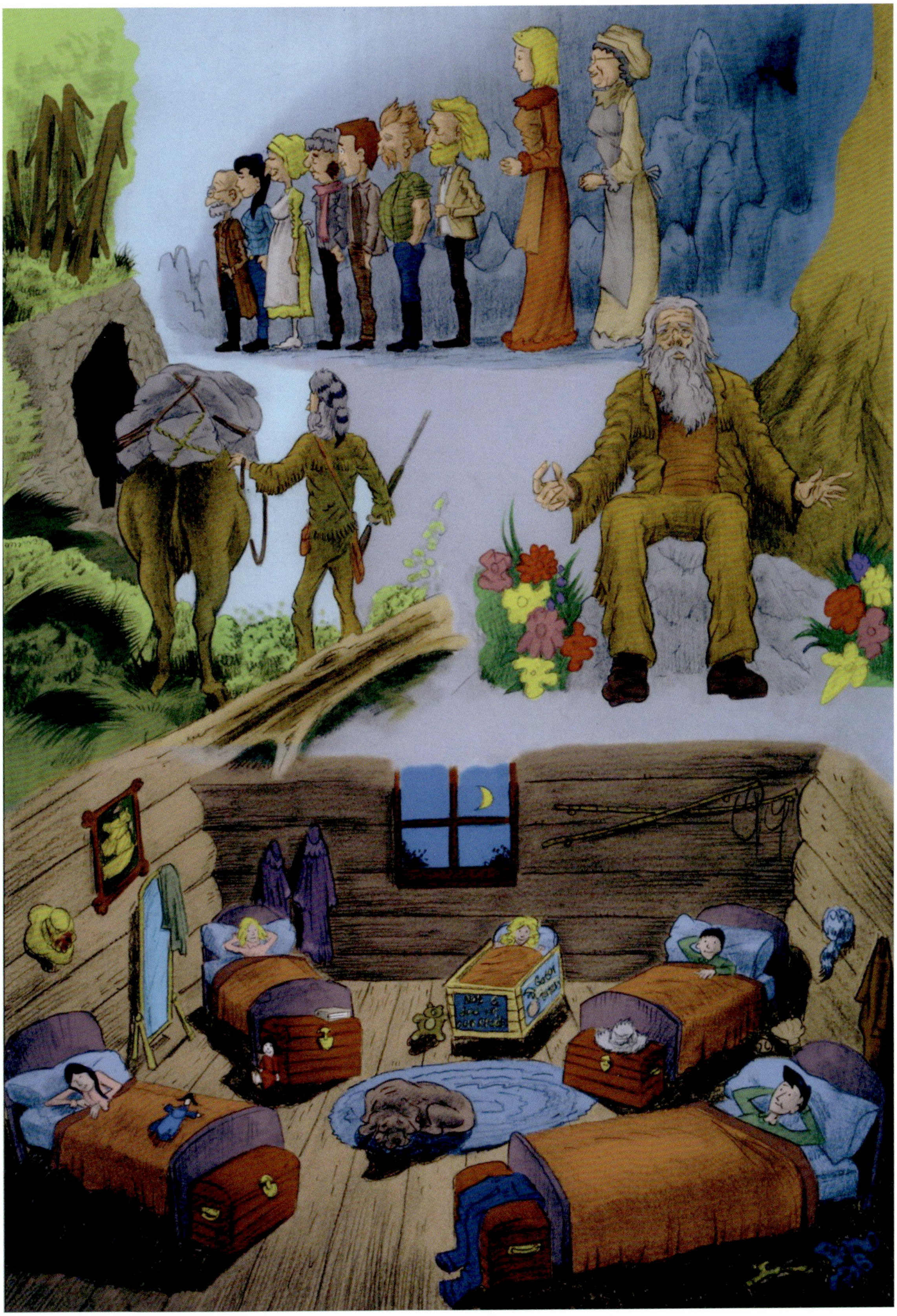

But...
for now they must stay quietly contented
With their new adventure up ol' Hermits Hill
But the Mugwhumps said someth'n quite reveal'n
Not allow'n the Bunches thoughts ta be peacefully still.

The Mugwhumps...
Mentioned an ol' burnt out hollowed oak tree
'n spoke of a shiny gold pirates front tooth
Were they know'nly lure'n them off the true trail
Or just maybe purposely expos'n the treasures real truth?

"Y'all a good night".

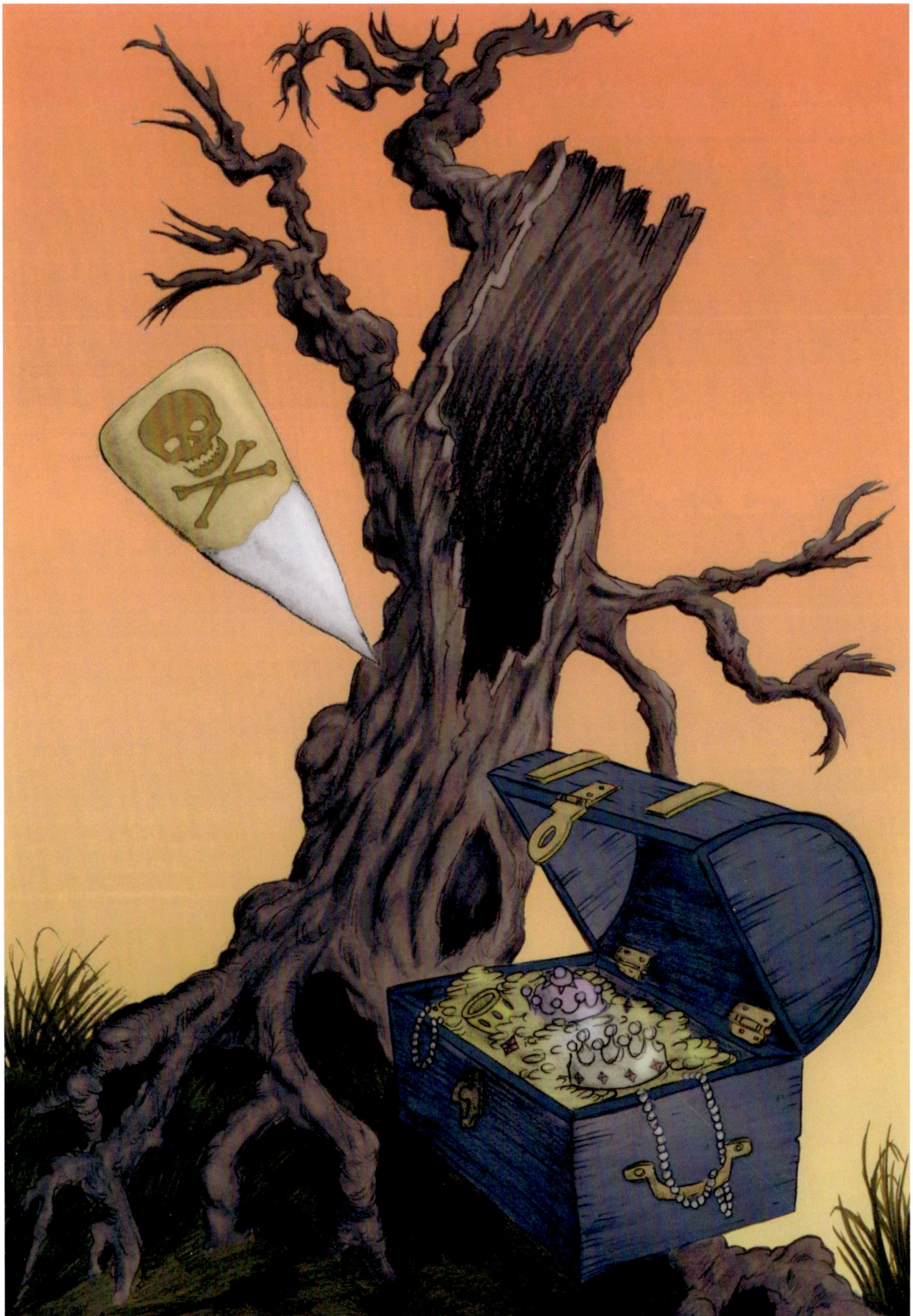

ISBN:978-0-9847480-0-6

ISBN:978-0-9847480-1-3